# Shivers

## THE SECRET OF FERN ISLAND

## M. D. Spenser

**Plantation, Florida**

Published by Paradise Press, Inc. by arrangement with River Publishing, Inc. All right, title and interest to the "SHIVERS" logo and design are owned by River Publishing, Inc. No portion of the "SHIVERS" logo and design may be reproduced in part or whole without prior written permission from River Publishing, Inc. An application for a registered trademark of the "SHIVERS" logo and design is pending with the Federal Patent and Trademark office.


ISBN 1-57657-056-8


EXCLUSIVE DISTRIBUTION BY PARADISE PRESS, INC.

Cover Design by George Paturzo
Cover Illustration by Eddie Roseboom


Printed in the U.S.A.

**30585**

**DO YOU ENJOY BEING FRIGHTENED?**

**WOULD YOU RATHER HAVE
NIGHTMARES
INSTEAD OF SWEET DREAMS?**

**ARE YOU HAPPY ONLY WHEN
SHAKING WITH FEAR?**

# CONGRATULATIONS ! ! ! !

**YOU'VE MADE A WISE CHOICE.**

**THIS BOOK IS THE DOORWAY
TO ALL THAT MAY FRIGHTEN YOU.**

**GET READY FOR**

## COLD, CLAMMY SHIVERS
**RUNNING UP AND DOWN YOUR SPINE!**

**NOW, OPEN THE DOOR—
IF YOU DARE ! ! ! !**

For Stephanie and Rebecca,
my favorite little girls

# THE SECRET OF
# OF
# FERN ISLAND

## **Chapter One**

"Don't even think about it, Kenny," Stephanie called to her friend, who had stopped by the sea, as usual. "I'm not going over there."

"I knew it!" Kenny yelled. "I told you he would be there. Man, I want to go over there and talk to him. Come *on*. Let's go!"

"No way," Stephanie said. "My father told me not to go near that bridge."

She toyed nervously with the streamers hanging from the handlebars of her new purple bicycle.

"Don't you want to talk to him?" asked Kenny.

He shaded his eyes and gazed across the water toward an island. A boy sat on the damp ground of the island, with his fishing pole in the air and the line plunged into the ocean.

"Come on, Steph," Kenny said. "Aren't you even a little bit curious? He's sitting there every time

1

we come by here. He's just a little boy. What can he do to us?"

"You know we're not supposed to cross that bridge," she said. "The sign says so. And my father doesn't want me over there. That bridge doesn't even look like it can hold us up."

"Then how did *he* get over there?" Kenny asked.

His voice softened as he tried to reason with Stephanie. She was one of his best friends in the world, even though she was a girl. She was eleven, like he was, and an adventurer, as well.

"Look how small he is," Kenny said. "We've got to be four or five years older than he is. What's he going to do? What could go wrong?"

Stephanie paused to think. She didn't really know the answer. Still, she felt that something could go wrong — even if she couldn't put her finger on what it was.

Fern Island had been closed to the public many years ago. Nobody lived there any more, and cars had ceased crossing the rickety bridge. Stephanie's father told her that even the scientists who had once reveled

2

in the island's luscious vegetation had stopped going to Fern Island.

A rusty metal chain and a sign warned them not to trespass.

"I don't know what could go wrong," Stephanie said. "And I don't want to find out. That boy looks strange. Look, he's got that stupid lantern with him again. I never knew anybody who wanted to fish all of the time like that. Let's go, Kenny. It's almost time for dinner."

"It will only take a few minutes," Kenny said. "We'll just run over there, talk to him for five minutes, and leave. We won't be late for dinner."

"We *will* be late, Kenny," Stephanie said. "It's not like we live just around the corner. And if I'm late, Mom won't let me ride tomorrow. You know that."

The island, surrounded by the sparkling blue of the ocean, sat in an inlet a full ten miles east of Cocoplum, the small community where Kenny and Stephanie lived. Stephanie's parents did not even allow her to ride that far on her bike alone — much less onto the forbidden island.

She worried that someone would see them

3

riding over to the island and turn them into the police. Or worse, their parents.

"Come on , Steph," Kenny coaxed. "Ten more minutes won't make that much of a difference. We'll ride home as fast as we can. And we'll go through the shortcuts."

Stephanie glanced quickly at the little boy on the island. He still sat in the same position, fishing, and acting like he did not even know they were there.

"I don't want to, Kenny," Stephanie said. "Please. It's time to go home. I just want to go back."

Kenny refused to give up.

"OK, what if we come back tomorrow and, if he's there, we'll talk to him then?" he asked. "I promise, nothing bad is going to happen."

"Why don't you just do it by yourself?" Stephanie asked.

"Because it'll be more fun if we do it to-gether," he said. "We'll just go and talk to him for a little while and then leave. Then we can go back to school and tell our friends. They'll be so jealous."

Stephanie was a tomboy — the only one in her class. The thought of having her own private adventure to tell her friends about appealed to her.

"All right," she said, at last. "But all we're going to do is talk to him, right? And then we'll go, right?"

"Yeah, of course," Kenny said. "As soon as you want to go, we'll leave."

"Cool. We can do that. Let's go home now."

Kenny raised the kickstand on his black mountain bike and pedaled off, leading the way back to Cocoplum. Stephanie mounted her bike and followed. She wondered whether the little boy would go home for dinner, too.

She looked over her shoulder one last time. The sun was setting, spreading an orange reflection across the sparkling sea. The shadows were growing longer. Evening was coming.

But the little boy on the island continued fishing, his lantern flickering beside him.

# Chapter Two

"Are you ready to go?" Kenny asked the second he heard Stephanie answer the telephone.

"Come on over," Stephanie said. "But I have to tell you something. My mom is making me take my sister with me today."

"I don't care," Kenny said.

"And her friend," Stephanie added.

"What friend?" Kenny asked, sounding worried.

"Her friend Brooksie is staying with us for two days because her parents are out of town. My mom had some things to do, and she asked me if they could come riding with us today. I didn't know what to say. I don't think we should go you-know-where today."

"What?" Kenny asked indignantly. "Steph, are you crazy? I've waited all day for this. You *told* me

6

we could go today. Why can't we take them? What's the difference?"

"Ken," Stephanie replied, annoyed. "I don't think I should take my sister over there."

"Becky's not a baby. She's nine years old — in the fourth grade already. What, are you still scared or something?"

Well, maybe she was — a little. But she had told her friend Rita she would cross the bridge to Fern Island that afternoon. Rita had been impressed.

Stephanie could not back out now. She'd look bad — and not quite as tomboyish as she wished.

"Oh, all right," she said. "Just come over here. I don't know what we're going to tell them. They'll have to keep their mouths shut."

# **Chapter Three**

The warm sun peeked through the clouds as they started their journey. Brooksie and Becky had both pulled their hair back into ponytails, which bounced on their necks as they pedaled.

Stephanie had not told them where they were going, but they didn't care. They were glad to be out riding with the older kids.

Kenny led the way, often veering at high speed up steep embankments alongside the road. The girls liked that. They giggled and rang their bells, and pretended they were going to crash into each other.

Stephanie said little. She kept thinking about the bridge and the boy who always fished on the forbidden island.

Becky started whining.

"Can we go to the park and feed the ducks?"

she asked. "I've got a cramp in my thigh."

"Oh, yeah, can we?" Brooksie echoed. "I've always wanted to have a duck for a pet, but my dad gave me a bunny instead."

"Yes!" Stephanie yelled back to them. Her stomach felt so jittery she was sure a swarm of caterpillars was writhing inside of it.

Kenny did not protest. While the girls fed the ducks, he rode off, popping wheelies all over the park.

The sun rose higher, and the air grew hotter and more humid. Kenny's T-shirt clung to his back. Sweat dripped from his forehead.

"Let's get some drinks and head on out of here!" Kenny yelled. "It's hotter'n a gosh-darned oven out here today."

Brooksie covered her mouth with her hand.

"Ooooh, you shouldn't say darn," she whispered under her breath. Then she  waved goodbye to the ducks and picked up her bicycle.

Becky quickly followed her and mounted her own.

Stephanie lingered behind to toss a penny into the pond and make a wish. She closed her eyes and wished with all her heart that the boy would not be fishing on the island today.

She had a vague feeling that something bad would happen if they crossed the bridge. Surely there was a reason it was closed.

But when they reached the shore, she looked out across the water, and her heart fell.

There sat the boy, in the same place they had seen him the night before, almost as if he had never moved.

# **Chapter Four**

He sat on the bank wearing the same T-shirt and the same jeans. His fishing line dangled into the water at exactly the same point.

"All *right*!" Kenny yelled, pointing across the bridge. "Come on, girls!"

"What's Kenny yelling about?" Becky asked. "It's only a bridge."

They were just fifteen feet from the Fern Island Bridge — and the sign warning against trespassers. Stephanie pulled up behind Kenny and looked over his shoulder.

As they watched, the boy gazed into the water as if he was looking for something he had lost. The muscles in Stephanie's stomach tightened.

"Do you guys know him?" Becky asked.

"No," Kenny replied. "But we're going to

11

meet him."

"Isn't this the bridge we're not supposed to cross?" Brooksie asked. "Isn't this the Fern Island Bridge?"

Stephanie looked down at her sneaker. She bent down to retie it while she waited for Kenny to respond.

"Um, yes, this is the Fern Island Bridge," he said. "We just want to go talk to that boy, and then we'll leave. There's nothing wrong with that."

Brooksie frowned.

"I don't want to cross that bridge," she said. "The sign says we can't go over there. Look at that bridge. It wobbles. I don't want to become a Weeble Wobble."

Becky laughed. She looked at the one-lane bridge. The guardrails were rusty, and the wood pilings were moldy and rotten. She wondered if her friend might have a point.

"Even if it was OK to go to Fern Island, we would never make it across the bridge," Brooksie continued. "My father told me that it's not strong enough to hold up even one car."

"Give me a break," Kenny said. "I know it's not the best bridge in the universe, but it's not that bad. Is your dad an engineer or something?"

"No, he's an artist."

"Stop it, you guys," Stephanie whispered. "I saw him move. I swear. He looked at us."

She moved close to Kenny, so that only he could hear her.

"He's still got that lantern," she whispered.

The lantern bothered Stephanie more than anything. Why did he need it in the daytime?

"Relax, Steph, everything's going to be OK," Kenny muttered, clenching his teeth. "Don't you trust me?"

"I don't think this is such a good idea," Stephanie said. "The girls don't seem like they want to do this. It's too weird, Kenny. How many boys do you know that fish all day every day, with lanterns next to them?"

"That's exactly why I want to meet him," Kenny said. "You *promised*, Steph. It's going to be fun. We might be the first kids on Fern Island. They might even put us on the six o'clock news."

Becky and Brooksie were straddling their bikes, feet on the ground, staring across the water at the boy. Stephanie turned around and spoke to them.

"Do you guys want to go?" she asked.

Becky shrugged.

"My dad will kill me if he finds out," Brooksie said.

"Yeah, but we don't have to tell him," Becky answered.

Stephanie's strategy wasn't working. She had hoped the younger girls would convince Kenny to abandon his plan. But the strange boy across the water had apparently piqued her little sister's curiosity.

"Don't pay attention to Kenny," Becky told Brooksie. "We're not going to be on the news. Nobody will know. We won't get in trouble."

"Oh, all right," Brooksie said. "We're not going to stay long, are we? We're supposed to be back before the sun goes down."

"I know," Stephanie chimed in. "We won't be long at *all*."

"He looked over here again!" Becky said, excitedly. "You think he wants us to go over there?"

14

"Let's get moving," Kenny said. "We'll go over the bridge one at a time, real slowly."

He stopped and put his finger to his lips while he thought it over.

"On second thought," he said, "why don't we walk our bikes over it? I'll be last. Come on, Steph, lead the way."

"Me?" Stephanie asked in alarm. "Why don't *you* go first?"

"I think I should stay behind in case any of you need any help crossing over."

"Why would we need help?" Stephanie asked. "What are you worried about? That it'll collapse?"

Kenny sighed and shook his head. Stephanie was not going to make this easy for him. He walked to the bridge, ducked under the chain and jumped hard on the planks.

The bridge shook, rippled, then stabilized and became still. Kenny jumped on it again.

"See? There's nothing to worry about!" he said.

"Stop being so chicken, Steph," Becky said. "This is going to be so cool!"

With a sigh of resignation, Stephanie walked her bike toward the bridge. She closed her eyes and wished the little boy would be gone when she opened them.

It didn't work. He was still there — still fishing. He seemed not to notice her. His lantern glimmered, though its light was barely visible in the midday sun.

She started to wheel her bike across the bridge. Kenny urged her to keep going. She did not look back.

The tattered bridge clanked under her feet. She could see the ocean between gaps in the planks — gaps which widened under her weight. The metal beams that held up the bridge were rusted and flaking.

The rocking of the bridge made her dizzy. She took a deep breath and forced herself to look straight ahead.

Finally she stepped onto solid ground, not sure whether she was glad to be off the bridge — or nervous, at long last, to actually set foot on Fern Island.

"Go, Becky," said Kenny. "One down, three more to go."

Becky crossed the bridge at a brisk pace, showing no signs of concern. Stephanie shook her head in wonder. She knew that Becky loved playing detective, and crossing over to Fern Island was probably her biggest mystery yet.

Still, Stephanie thought, you'd think she'd be at least a *little* nervous.

"Slow down!" Kenny yelled. "You're going too fast."

The bridge swung under Becky's steps. Two of the planks cracked open, and the front wheel of Becky's bike got stuck. She pushed with all of her strength, but her bike would not budge.

She pushed so hard she slipped and almost fell from the bridge.

"Watch out!" Stephanie yelled.

She ran to the bridge to help Becky. Her heart pounded. Becky looked at her with frightened eyes.

"Grab the handlebar and pull the bike up," Stephanie cried. "You're not going to fall. You just need to get the wheel out of the crack!"

Becky did as she was told. Within a minute, she was at her sister's side, gasping for air. Stephanie put her arm around her sister's shoulders as they waited for the others.

"Go slow," Kenny warned Brooksie. "Don't act crazy, like Becky. I *told* you guys we have to go slow."

Brooksie didn't need to be told twice.

"I can't wait for this to be over," she muttered.

She gripped her handlebars so tightly her knuckles went white. She looked as if she was holding her breath.

"Stay over to the right," Stephanie yelled. "You don't want to get stuck over where Becky did."

Brooksie inched her bike slowly toward the right edge of the bridge. She kept her gaze straight ahead, never once looking down.

"He got up!" Stephanie yelled. "He's up, Kenny. He's up!"

Kenny ran to the bridge's edge. The little boy stood looking at Stephanie and Becky. Stephanie stared back at him.

Again, she closed her eyes and wished he would disappear. Again, it failed to work. When she opened her eyes this time, the boy stood there still —

18

eerily quiet, saying nothing, just looking.

Stephanie turned back to the bridge. Brooksie wheeled her bike onto the island and breathed a sigh of relief.

Kenny grabbed his bike and began to walk it across the bridge.

Stephanie looked back at the little boy. He stood straight, staring not at them any longer, but at the water. His lantern and fishing pole lay on the ground beside him.

But when they started walking toward him, he angrily snatched his pole and his lantern off the ground and darted off towards the woods.

"Let's go after him!" Kenny said. He mounted his bike and motioned the others to follow him.

But the boy had disappeared.

# Chapter Five

It was difficult to steer the bicycles through the tall blades of grass.

Lush greenery covered the ground — grass, thistles, dandelions, bushes, trees, and ferns in abundance. Kenny and the girls could see where Fern Island had gotten its name.

Kenny scoured the woods for some sign of the boy. The woods ahead were dark, and the boy had vanished into them. Suddenly, he started pedaling even faster.

"I see his lantern," he called back over his shoulder. "Come on, you guys! I don't want to lose him!"

Stephanie looked back at Becky and Brooksie. Both were struggling with their pedals. Stephanie stopped to pull burs off her socks. She leaned too much to one side and fell. Her bicycle landed on top of her.

Becky and Brooksie giggled and helped her get up. Then they heard Kenny yell in frustration.

"Oh no, he's gone!" Kenny said. "I can't believe we lost him. He's on *foot* for goodness sake!"

Stephanie wiped her hands on her shorts and ignored Kenny. Secretly, she was glad the boy had disappeared. Maybe now they could go home.

"Hurry *up* you guys," Kenny called. "Come on!"

"Let's just go home, Kenny," Stephanie said. "He doesn't want to talk to us. Why should we chase him?"

Kenny turned around and pedaled back toward the girls.

"Aren't you the least bit curious?" he asked. "He probably ran because he thinks we're going to hurt him. When he realizes we just want to be his friends, he'll talk to us. You'll see."

"I'm tired," Stephanie said. "I want to go home."

"What about you guys?" Kenny asked, turning

toward Becky and Brooksie. Brooksie started to agree with Stephanie, but Becky interrupted.

"We want to keep going," she said loudly. "We've come too far to stop now."

Brooksie frowned, but she did not complain. Stephanie frowned, too. That was just like Becky — she wanted to press ahead to solve the mystery, no matter what.

"I don't care what you guys say," Stephanie said. "I'm not staying."

Just then, Stephanie thought she saw a light twinkling between the trees. She looked again, but it was gone.

"Becky, let's go," she said. "I can't go home without you guys. Kenny can stay here if he wants to."

Again, a light flashed through a gap in the ferns. This time, Kenny saw it too. The boy dodged through the underbrush.

"He's back, he's back!" Kenny shouted. "Now's our chance!"

He pedaled furiously towards the light. Becky and Brooksie jumped on their bikes and rushed after him. Stephanie had no choice but to follow.

She cast a glance behind her as she rode. The bridge was no longer visible.

The bikes ahead of her disappeared into the woods, following a trail lined with scrub and foliage. She found riding the trail tricky and difficult. It wound its way around roots and over rocks. Sometimes, she thought she was lost.

But always the lantern flickered in front of them, leading the way.

*       *       *

On this side of Fern Island, the ocean was prettier, calmer and seemed more blue. Hills of sand sculpted by the winds gave the island a peaceful feeling.

Stephanie liked this side much better than the other. The fresh breeze made her want to sink into the sand and build castles.

But she knew better. They were on a mission.

An imposing, black lighthouse stood at the end of the island. Stephanie's father had told her stories of pirates who had gotten lost at sea and used lighthouses to guide them. She wondered if there were any pirates in this lighthouse.

"Did you know there was a lighthouse on this island?" she asked Kenny.

"No," he said. "Did you?"

"I don't think so," Stephanie said. "My dad never told me about it. Maybe he doesn't know it. You think they still use it?"

"I doubt it," Kenny said. "It doesn't seem like anyone comes around here anymore. The island seems totally deserted, doesn't it?"

"Yeah, it sure does," Stephanie said.

They looked around — at the sea, the sand, the lighthouse, the woods. Just when they had thought they were catching up to the boy, his lantern had winked out and he had given them the slip.

They stood and watched the surf a moment. The place seemed so peaceful. The only sounds were the swish of the waves on the sand, the whispering of the wind in the leaves, the calls of the birds in the trees — and Brooksie, who suddenly began to yell like crazy.

"I see him! I see him!" she shouted.

The others swiveled their heads, but saw nothing.

"He was looking at us from behind those bushes," Brooksie said breathlessly. "I saw the lantern, and he saw me. He took off that way. He ran toward the lighthouse!"

Kenny grabbed his bike and sped off as fast as he could ride over the caked sand of the beach. He reached the lighthouse ahead of the rest of them, and stood there waiting impatiently while the others caught up.

"He's in there," he said. "I saw him. Let's go inside!"

"All right," Stephanie said. "But if he doesn't want to talk, we're leaving, right?"

"That was the deal," Kenny answered.

They leaned their bikes against a fence and pulled the door open.

Inside the lighthouse, it was dark and cold and quiet. The door slammed shut behind them. Brooksie bumped into a black steel chair by a window. The bang echoed loudly, bouncing around and around the metal walls of the hollow building.

"Oops," she said.

"Shhhhh," Kenny said. "We don't want him to get scared."

"We don't want *him* to get scared?" Stephanie asked. "Who are you kidding?"

"There's not much in here, is there?" Becky said. "Maybe there's more stuff upstairs."

Each tiny sound echoed and grew until it filled the building. Stephanie found herself walking on tiptoe without even thinking about it.

"I doubt there's anything up there," she said. "I don't think anyone's been here in ages."

She touched the window sill. Her finger was smudged with a thick, black layer of dust.

"That's disgusting," she said.

A spiral staircase loomed in front of them, rising in ever-narrowing circles to the top of the lighthouse. Kenny pointed to it.

"He's gotta be up there," he whispered. "Let's go on up."

"What for?" Stephanie asked. "This kid does not want to talk to us. Why should we chase him up there?"

"We're not *chasing* him," Kenny said. "We're not going to *do* anything to him. If he tells us to leave, we'll go."

Kenny climbed up a few steps and looked back at the girls.

"Come on you guys," he whispered, beckoning to them. "We're already here!"

The girls followed — first Becky, then Brooksie. Stephanie brought up the rear.

The four of them climbed in circles, trying hard to be quiet as they stepped on the metal stairs.

"Man, there's a lot of steps on this thing," said Becky. "Where are we going — to the sky?"

"Shhhhhh," Brooksie said. "You want him to hear us?"

Suddenly, Stephanie's right hand began to itch. She brought it to her face to study it in the dim light.

A spider's web was wrapped around her hand.

"Oh, yuck," she cried, and the words echoed around and around. "Help me get this thing off of me!"

"Will you guys shut up?" Kenny said, clenching his teeth.

The girls collected themselves and continued to climb. Stephanie kept picturing spiders crawling all over her body. She felt so tense her muscles ached.

After what seemed like a hundred steps — maybe more — they reached the top.

They emerged into a big room with one large bay window that looked out over the ocean. Sunlight streamed in through the window, brightening the room and offering welcome relief from the dark and damp of the staircase.

Stephanie started to breathe more easily. She felt her shoulders relax, just a bit.

The room was quiet, except for the whistling of the wind outside — stronger at this height, it seemed, than it was at ground level.

The room was empty. The little boy was nowhere to be seen.

But there, on a table in the middle of the room, his lantern sat, still glowing.

# **Chapter Six**

"Look," Kenny said, walking over to the table. "His lantern is here. He's got to be here someplace."

Stephanie examined the lantern. The outside of it looked like it was crusted over with something. Inside, the flame flickered and winked.

Stephanie felt uneasy. She desperately wanted Kenny to give up the chase. This trip was far more than she had bargained for.

"He doesn't want to talk to us," she said. "Can't you get that through your thick skull?"

"Hush up, Steph," he said. "He *has* to be here somewhere. There's no way he could have left the lighthouse without running into us."

Becky and Brooksie paid no attention to their conversation. They busily inspected the dusty pictures that hung on the walls, and the stained and faded newspapers that covered part of the floor.

A small clock with only one hand rested against a back wall. A trail of cracker crumbs led to a cracked window.

"You think he *lives* here?" Brooksie asked Becky.

Becky's eyes widened at the thought.

A painting of a shipwreck, which hung upside down on a wall, drew Brooksie's attention, and she looked at it more closely.

"Ooooh, that's creepy," she said. "There's a skeleton driving this ship!"

Becky hurried over to look.

"He's smiling," Becky said. "That *is* creepy. I wonder why it's upside down. This place is making me shiver."

Stephanie walked over to see for herself. She grabbed the picture, turned it right side up, and stepped back to look at it.

Within seconds, the picture turned itself upside down again.

"Whoa!" Brooksie said. "Did you see that?"

"That's nothing," Becky said. "The pictures at

my house do the same thing. After my mom dusts them, they never stay up straight."

Stephanie's stomach did somersaults. She heard what her little sister said, but she disagreed. A tilted picture was one thing. But a picture turning itself around at will?

She took three deep breaths and tried to calm down. Maybe, she told herself, she hadn't just seen what she thought she'd seen.

She turned away. Kenny was standing by the window.

"What are you doing over there?" she asked.

"I was just wondering how he got out of here without us seeing him," Kenny said. "It makes no sense."

"Look you guys," Brooksie said. She pointed to two mossy fishing poles that lay on the floor. "I bet these are his."

Kenny grabbed the poles and pretended to throw a line.

"These are nasty," he said, wiping his hands on his pants. "Why would anyone want to fish with these?"

"Why would anyone want to be here at all?" Stephanie said sharply. The rotating picture had upset her badly, and she was growing more and more annoyed that her desire to leave was being ignored.

"I'm going to go downstairs and see if he's down there. Maybe we just missed him," Kenny said.

"No," Stephanie said. "We're *all* going downstairs. And then we're leaving!"

"Steph, give me a chance," Kenny said. "We're already here. I won't be long."

Stephanie plopped down angrily and sat on the frigid floor with her legs crossed and her head down. She was so sick of this adventure that she did not care how grimy the floor was. She looked at the newspapers spread here and there, but did not pick them up.

"Hey, Steph, there's a door over here," Brooksie said from the back of the room. "You think it leads to another room or something?"

"Who cares?" Stephanie snapped. "This place gives me the creeps."

But Becky was interested, of course. It really stank, Stephanie thought, having a daredevil detective for a little sister.

Becky and Brooksie opened the door. It creaked heavily. Behind it they found a small closet full of old junk — a few bald tires, some tools, and an old chest.

Becky pulled the top of the chest open and peered inside.

"There's nothing interesting in here," she said, and started to leave.

But as she walked out of the closet, Brooksie grabbed her shoulder.

Becky turned around and gasped. Stephanie heard her and scrambled off the floor to come take a look.

On a shelf in the closet, a silver phonograph spun an old vinyl record around and around and around. The needle sat in its holder, not on the record. Still, when they listened closely, they heard gurgling sounds. It sounded like a melody, but they could not make out the tune. It made no sense.

Outside, the wind whistled louder around the lighthouse.

Stephanie and the girls bent close to the old phonograph to listen more carefully. This was no music. Was the record player broken? How could it play anything if the needle was not on the record?

Suddenly, the sound grew louder.

The girls stepped back in shock.

The phonograph spoke louder, and louder still, until it nearly shouted the words: "SWIM . . . YOU . . . CAN? . . . SWIM . . . YOU . . . CAN? . . . SWIM . . . YOU . . . CAN?"

# **Chapter Seven**

"What does that mean?" Becky asked.

Brooksie looked too astonished to speak. Stephanie's mouth hung open in amazement.

She moved her lips, but no sound came out. Finally, she found her voice — or at least part of it.

"That ancient record player," she croaked. "Did it just play by itself?"

Before anyone could answer, they heard a short scream from downstairs, followed by heavy footsteps.

"Kenny?" Stephanie yelled. "Kenny?"

There was no answer.

"He probably can't hear us because the door is closed," Becky said. "Open it and take a look."

"Are you crazy?" Stephanie shot back.

"What if Kenny's in trouble?" Becky asked.

She walked to the door, cupped her hand over her ear and leaned against it.

"You hear anything?" Brooksie asked. Becky signaled her to be quiet.

Brooksie and Stephanie leaned close to the door, too. They heard nothing — not the slightest sound that could let them know whether it was safe to open the door.

"What we need to do," said Becky, "is open the door very quietly and see what's going on. We have to investigate. Kenny might need us."

"Maybe we should call out his name again," Stephanie said. "KEN — "

Becky lunged at Stephanie and clamped her hand over her mouth.

"Stop doing that!" she hissed. "If something is wrong, we don't want to give away that we're up here!"

Suddenly, heavy footsteps startled the girls again. THUMP! THUMP! THUMP!

"Oh, no!" Brooksie whispered, her hands flying to her face. "He's coming up here!"

Then the thumps stopped. An eerie quiet filled

36

the lighthouse.

"He's *not* coming up here," Becky said. "What's going on?"

"This is really starting to scare me," Stephanie said, her voice starting to shake. "I just want to get out of here. I can't wait for Kenny to come back."

"*If* he comes back," Brooksie said.

Stephanie gave her little sister a worried look.

"I *knew* we shouldn't have done this," she said. "As soon as the coast is clear, we are getting out of here."

She looked wildly around the room. There was no other way out, of course — not from the top of a lighthouse. They were trapped.

The lantern on the table flickered and caught her eye. She felt an urge to go turn it off, but she stopped herself. She thought she should stay near the door.

The phonograph started playing again, even louder than before, booming at them in an oily male voice: "SWIM . . . YOU . . . CAN? . . . SWIM . . . YOU . . . CAN? . . . SWIM . . . YOU . . . CAN?"

"What does that *mean*?" Becky asked again.

Warily, the girls approached the ancient record player.

"Maybe it doesn't mean anything," Stephanie said. On an impulse, she picked up the needle and placed it on the record.

To her horror, the needle lifted itself back up and replaced itself in its holder.

"We gotta get out of here," Stephanie said. "We have got to get out of here."

"SWIM YOU CAN?" the machine asked again, and then fell silent.

Stephanie hugged herself. Becky and Brooksie hugged each other.

All of a sudden, the door flew open and smashed against the wall behind it.

Becky and Brooksie bumped heads as they both tried to run in the same direction. Stephanie stood frozen by the phonograph.

Someone was coming into the room!

# Chapter Eight

"What the heck is the matter with you guys?" Kenny asked. He stood just inside the door at the top of the staircase, breathing heavily and soaked with sweat.

"What is wrong with *you*?" Stephanie snapped. "You scared us half to death."

"Well, excuse me," Kenny said. "I was just trying to get up here as fast as I could."

"What happened downstairs?" Becky asked. Brooksie walked over and shut the door again.

"I looked everywhere," Kenny said. "I can't imagine where he went. It's like he vanished or something."

"He probably went fishing," Stephanie answered testily.

"I doubt that," Kenny replied.

"We heard someone scream," Becky said.

"That was me," Kenny said. "Be glad you guys didn't go down there with me. I found a secret door behind the bottom of the stairwell. I thought maybe he was hiding in there. What I found was a bunch of bats wanting someone to play with."

"What?" Brooksie asked. "There's bats in here?"

"Yeah, big ones, too," Kenny replied.

"Can we just *leave*?" Stephanie said. "This place is getting scarier every second."

Kenny sighed and rolled his eyes.

"The bats are in that little room downstairs," he explained, with exaggerated patience. "They're not up here."

"No," said Brooksie. "But we have something just as strange up here — or even stranger."

She walked over to the phonograph. Kenny wiped the sweat off his forehead with his sleeve and followed her toward the closet.

"This old record player makes very eerie noises," she said.

"Like what?"

"It gurgles and it says things to us that don't make any sense. It asks us questions," Brooksie said.

"You guys are nuts," Kenny said.

"No, it really does," Stephanie said. "I really think it's trying to communicate with us."

Kenny laughed.

"Very funny," he said. "But the bats are real."

"Kenny, we're not joking," Stephanie said sharply.

"Of course you're not," Kenny said. "Come on, you guys. I really saw the bats. They scared the living daylights out of me, which is why I yelled. But you want me to believe this old, broken record player is talking to you? You could make up a better story than that."

"Oh, forget it," Brooksie said. "What's the use? If all you're going to do is make fun of us, forget we ever said anything."

"Let's forget the whole thing and get out of here," Stephanie said, heading for the door. "Come on, you guys."

"Wait!" Kenny said. "We haven't talked to him yet. After all we've been through, you guys are willing

41

to give up without talking to him?"

"Yes!" the three girls shot back.

A shadow flitted quickly across the window. Stephanie saw it out of the corner of her eye. She turned to look, but the shadow was gone. She decided she had imagined it. This place gave her the creeps.

But the shadow moved across the window again — more slowly this time. It darkened more than half the window.

Stephanie swallowed hard and shivered.

"Did you see that?" Kenny asked. Stephanie nodded.

"It must have been a bird," she said hopefully.

Kenny walked past her to the window. He craned his neck this way and that, but saw nothing.

"Kenny, I want to go," Stephanie said. Her voice cracked, and her eyes moistened with tears.

Kenny put his arm around her.

"Steph, don't cry," he said softly. "I didn't mean to upset you. I thought this would be fun."

Stephanie rested her head on Kenny's shoulder and closed her eyes. She imagined herself at home in her cozy bedroom. Back where everything was safe, and strange shadows never moved across the windows, and her CD player never talked on its own.

Kenny chewed his fingertips.

They heard a tap on the window.

Stephanie looked up. In the window, she saw a baseball cap.

The little boy was back!

# **Chapter Nine**

The boy stared through the window at them with no expression on his face.

Kenny was speechless. Stephanie was wide-eyed with shock.

The boy stared and stared.

"Kenny, say something to him," Stephanie urged.

Kenny started to talk, but no sounds came out of his mouth. The boy stared at them for a few more seconds, and then disappeared. Just like that, he was gone!

Kenny rubbed his eyes and looked again. Stephanie just stared, with her mouth hanging open, at the place where the boy had been.

She saw nothing but clouds and sea and sky.

"But how?" Kenny said finally. "Was he just

hanging in the air?"

Stephanie was shaking. She hugged her arms around herself and trembled.

"I want to go now!" she shouted.

Kenny said nothing. He pressed his nose against the window again, but the boy was gone.

Becky and Brooksie moved closer to the window.

"Was it him?" Becky asked. "What's going on?"

"NOTHING!" Stephanie yelled. "LET'S GET OUT OF HERE NOW!"

Kenny ran his fingers through his hair and took a deep breath.

"Maybe that was just a weird shadow or something," he said. He did not sound convinced.

"A shadow of what, Kenny?" Stephanie asked angrily. "Do you know how high we are? What do you think it was — a bird that *looks* like that stupid little boy?"

Suddenly, the record player began talking again.

"DOWN ... FALLING ... IS ... BRIDGE .

.. ISLAND . . . FERN," it said.

Stephanie whirled around to face the machine. The record was spinning furiously. Over and over, louder and louder, the machine said, "DOWN . . . FALLING . . . IS . . . BRIDGE . . . ISLAND . . . FERN."

"What does that *mean*?" Becky asked.

"Listen," Kenny said. "You guys stay here and try to figure out the record player. I'm going to go back downstairs to find that boy."

"Are you crazy?" Stephanie yelled. "I want to go home, Kenny! You can't make us stay here forever."

"Steph, calm down," Kenny said. "I promise I won't be gone long. I have to figure this out. I can't go home without seeing that boy again. I just can't."

Stephanie narrowed her eyes and crossed her arms. This is the last time I will ever do anything like this, she told herself.

Kenny opened the door and walked out. The girls were alone again with the talking phonograph.

46

Stephanie pulled a chair out from the table and sat down. Face-to-face with the lantern, she started to cry.

# Chapter Ten

Stephanie's tears frightened Brooksie and Becky.

Not that they weren't frightened enough as it was. Stephanie knew that they looked up to her, because she was older. If she had stayed calm, the smaller girls might have calmed their own fears.

But Stephanie could not help herself. She had never felt so scared and trapped and helpless in all her life. She looked at the lantern, and the tears streamed down her face.

Becky and Brooksie hovered around her awkwardly. Becky paced around the table. Brooksie chewed on her thumbnail.

"Come on, Steph, don't cry," Brooksie told her. "As soon as Kenny comes back, we'll get out of here."

"Maybe we should just go downstairs now," Becky said. "We could wait for him where the bikes are."

"I don't know," Stephanie said. "What if we don't see him? What if something happens to him? I don't think we should go anywhere right now."

Becky picked up the lantern and held it close to her face. She tried to blow out the light. The flame flickered, nearly died, then glowed brightly again.

Becky blew at it again. Again the flame faltered, winked out, then leapt back to life.

"Leave that thing alone," Stephanie said, grabbing the lantern from her sister's hands. "You're going to get burned. We really shouldn't touch anything in here."

"Get burned?" Becky said. "That thing is ice cold, just like this room is."

Becky was right, Stephanie thought, looking at the lantern in her hands. The flame burned brightly inside, but the lantern was oddly cold.

Behind them, the record player began again its eerie speech.

"DOWN . . . FALLING . . . IS . . . BRIDGE .

. . ISLAND . . . FERN," it said.

"I'm getting ready to go break that thing," Becky said.

Becky sat on the cold floor with her legs crossed. She rubbed her face with her hands and started looking at the newspapers that were strewn about.

Stephanie looked down at her. That was Becky, she thought — always the detective no matter how frightening things got.

The newspapers had grown yellow with time. Some of the pages were muddy. Stephanie wondered why they were there. Was the little boy using them to wrap dead fish?

Becky started looking through the pages. Her face screwed up in concentration, and wrinkles creased her forehead.

"I think this newspaper is from another country or something," she said.

Brooksie walked over and sat down next to her. Together, they skimmed the pages.

"It looks like English," Brooksie said. "But I can't read it either."

Stephanie got down off her chair for a closer look. Next to one of the stories was a photograph of a woman holding a child in one arm and a pole in her free hand. But the article next to it was illegible. The words had no rhyme or reason, no order or sense.

"Is that a fishing pole?" Brooksie asked.

"It sure is," Stephanie said.

"I guess people used to do a lot of fishing around here," Brooksie said.

"You don't even know if that article is from here," Becky said. "You can't understand a word of it."

"Nothing in this dump makes any sense," Brooksie said angrily. "When is Kenny going to come back?"

Stephanie began to cry again. She dropped her face into her hands.

"I just want to go," she said to herself.

"You want to leave without Kenny?" Becky asked her.

Stephanie shook her head. She wished she had the courage to leave without Kenny. But she did not.

"Doesn't this look like the bridge we crossed

51

over?" Brooksie asked Becky. She showed Becky a photograph on a newspaper page.

"It sure does," Becky said. "That looks like the Fern Island Bridge. That picture must have been taken ages ago."

"I wish I knew how old this paper was," Brooksie said. The two girls scanned the pages for a date, but couldn't find one. Most of the printing was smudged.

"Look at that woman's hair-do," Brooksie said. "This is definitely old stuff."

"*Really* old," Becky said.

"But if that's a picture of the Fern Island Bridge, why aren't the words in English?" Brooksie asked.

"Beats me," Becky replied. "But you can tell the picture was taken when the bridge looked nicer. People probably walked over it all of the time way back then."

"My dad told me that people used to live on Fern Island a long time ago, but nobody lives here anymore," Brooksie said.

"It sure looked deserted when we rode over

here," Becky said.

"I think that cars used to cross on the bridge," Brooksie continued.

"Well, they don't anymore," Becky said. "If they did, they'd fall through for sure. We almost didn't make it."

"You mean *you* almost didn't make it," Brooksie said. "I wonder if there's a picture of the lighthouse in here."

The record player interrupted their chatter.

"DOWN . . . FALLING . . . IS . . . BRIDGE . . . ISLAND . . . FERN," it said.

Stephanie got up and walked toward the phonograph. She watched it spin in silence. Then it gurgled and began speaking again.

Over and over again, it repeated the same sounds:

"DOWN . . . FALLING . . . IS . . . BRIDGE . . . ISLAND . . . FERN."

"Stop it!" Stephanie yelled. "Stop it! Stop it!"

She picked up the needle and let it fall hard on the record. The scratching noise made the hairs on her arm stand up. Within seconds, the needle put itself back in its place.

Stephanie tried to yank the record off the turntable, but it would not come loose.

"Who knows how long it's been on there?" Brooksie said. "It's starting to feel like we've gone back in time or something."

"What do you mean?" Stephanie asked.

"I don't know," Brooksie said. "The record player is old. Everything in here seems like it's from another time. The newspapers are old. And look at the lantern. It seems like it's a hundred years old. It's all worn out. I'm surprised it even lights up."

Stephanie opened her eyes wide, stared at Brooksie, and bit her lip.

"You guys," she said. "We have got to go find Kenny."

# Chapter Eleven

They started descending the long staircase, spiraling their way down the long, hollow, echoing lighthouse.

Stephanie led the way. Becky followed. Brooksie brought up the rear.

They had forgotten how dark and dank the lighthouse was. They felt their way along while their eyes adjusted to the darkness.

"Kenny?" Stephanie called. She received no response, and her voice echoed so loudly that it startled her. She decided not to call out any more. Maybe Kenny was at the bottom of the staircase, checking out the room behind the secret door he'd discovered.

The room with the bats. Stephanie hoped Kenny had closed the door.

Their footsteps clanked and vibrated.

They were halfway down the stairs when they heard a rumble below them. Stephanie bent over the railing to look, but she saw nothing.

She waited a few seconds before tiptoeing down the stairs again. When she reached the bottom, she found no one — neither Kenny nor the little fisher-boy. She motioned to the smaller girls to be quiet.

Looking around, she saw the secret door Kenny had described. Behind it, she thought she heard the high-pitched squeal of bats. She wanted desperately to find Kenny, even if she had to drag him off this island — but that was one door she was not going to open.

Suddenly, she heard a bang on the window. She looked outside, but saw nothing but bushes.

Becky and Brooksie stood beside her, looking around and obeying her command to be quiet. Stephanie realized that she had somehow become the leader of this expedition. Her tears had dried, and the younger girls looked to her for guidance.

Suddenly, she felt the hair on the back of her neck prickle and stand up. Somebody, she was sure, was watching them.

A door slammed. Stephanie looked up. She could not believe her eyes.

There stood the little boy, not five feet away. The two of them stood face-to-face, staring at each other. Becky and Brooksie moved behind Stephanie and peeked out around her sides.

Stephanie stepped closer to the boy.

"Hi!" she said.

The boy squinted and stepped closer to her. He said nothing.

"Do you live here?" Stephanie asked.

The boy took a few more steps toward her. His face was manly and rigid. Stephanie's heart pounded so loud she could almost hear it.

"What's your name?" Stephanie asked. "I'm Stephanie."

The boy said nothing. Stephanie inched backward a step. The younger girls stayed behind her.

The boy walked forward and stopped directly in front of her.

"Say something," Stephanie urged him. The boy's head barely reached as high as her shoulders.

The boy said nothing and remained stone-faced. Stephanie extended her right hand, offering the boy a handshake, but the boy kept his hands to himself.

"We just wanted to meet you," Stephanie said.

The boy made no response. His dark eyes narrowed. His face grew meaner. Every time Stephanie stepped backward, the boy stepped forward. Soon, she and the younger girls were backed up against the wall of the lighthouse.

"We just want to be friends," Stephanie tried. She reached out to reassure the boy by patting him on the shoulder.

"Aaaaaggghhh!" she screamed, so loudly the younger girls jumped.

Her hand had gone right through the boy's shoulder.

The boy's eyes shifted. Stephanie began to panic. She reached out and touched the boy's other sleeve. Her hand passed through it as it would pass through a cloud.

Stephanie's knees buckled. The boy smirked and took off running. He opened the front door and bolted without looking back.

Stephanie ran outside, but she could not catch up with him. He disappeared into the woods.

She turned back to the lighthouse. The girls waited beside the lighthouse door. Kenny had joined them, wearing a scowl.

# Chapter Twelve

"I couldn't find him anywhere," Kenny said. "I looked all over the place."

He was hot and sweaty and looked very disappointed.

"Be glad you didn't," Stephanie said. "We did."

"What?" Kenny demanded. "When? Where? What'd he say?"

"He didn't want to talk," said Stephanie. "I'll tell you all about it — as soon as we leave this island."

She looked at Kenny triumphantly. She held all the cards now. If he wanted to hear about the boy, he would have to leave. They had to go home. This place was eerie and frightening. They should never have come in the first place, let alone brought the little girls.

"Oh, all right," Kenny spat. "Let's go." He stomped off toward his bike.

"We can't leave," said Becky.

"Can't?" Stephanie asked. "Why not?"

"Because I left my shoes upstairs."

Stephanie's heart fell. Becky was forever taking her shoes off and leaving them places. Part of her detective work, it seemed, was seeing how things felt in her bare feet.

Stephanie grimaced. Climbing to the top of the lighthouse, with its twirling pictures and talking record players, was the last thing she wanted to do. Nor did she desire any more encounters with little boys you could put your hand through.

"I thought we were getting out of here," she muttered under her breath.

Kenny, however, smiled. He had one more chance to find the little boy himself.

Silently, they climbed the spiral staircase, around and around and around. They saw no sign of the boy.

When they reached the sunlit room at the top of the lighthouse, they found Becky's shoes in the middle of the floor, right where she had been sitting to study the newspapers.

Suddenly, the record player buzzed. All four of them froze, and listened.

Loudly, the oily male voice spoke to them.

"FISHERMAN . . . A . . . KNOT . . . IS . . . HE!" it boomed. "FISHERMAN . . . A . . . KNOT . . . IS . . . HE! . . . FISHERMAN . . . A . . . KNOT . . . IS . . . HE!"

"Shut up!" Stephanie yelled. She slammed the closet door closed.

"Put your shoes on!" she shouted at her little sister, louder than she intended to. "Now! Now!"

From behind the closet door, its voice muted somewhat, the record player spoke to them still: Over and over again, it said: "FISHERMAN . . . A . . . KNOT . . . IS . . . HE!"

"What does that *mean*?" Becky asked.

"Put your shoes on!" Stephanie said. "It's trying to tell you to sit down and lace up your gosh-darned shoes. *Now*!" Stephanie said.

Brooksie covered her mouth with her hand.

"Ooooh, you shouldn't say darn," she whispered under her breath.

As Becky tied her shoes, Brooksie wandered

toward the closet.

"Don't you dare open that door!" Stephanie said.

"Why not?" Brooksie asked. "It doesn't make any difference. It's still talking."

She opened the door and touched the needle. The record continued spinning and hissing. She turned the volume knob, but nothing happened. The sound level remained the same.

"FISHERMAN . . . A . . . KNOT . . . IS . . . HE!" the record player sputtered again. "FISHERMAN . . . A . . . KNOT . . . IS . . . HE!"

"I really think it's trying to tell us something," Brooksie said.

"Something about fishermen and knots," Stephanie said. "Now let's get out of here."

Brooksie was deep in thought. Deciphering puzzles was her favorite pastime, and she was working on one now. She seemed not even to hear Stephanie.

"It's talking about a fisherman and that boy is always fishing," she said slowly. "I think there's a connection."

"FISHERMAN . . . A . . . KNOT . . . IS . . .

HE!" the phonograph sputtered.

Becky finished tying one shoe and started thumbing through the newspapers on the floor again.

Stephanie tapped her foot impatiently. But Kenny seemed in no hurry to leave. He looked out the window and down the staircase, apparently hoping the little boy would show up again.

"FISHERMAN . . . A . . . KNOT . . . IS . . . HE!" the phonograph announced.

## Chapter Thirteen

"What does that *mean?*" Becky asked.

Brooksie was still puzzling over the mystery.

"Fisherman a knot is he," she said to herself. "Fisherman a knot is he. That has to mean something. But how can somebody be a knot?"

Stephanie put her hands to her temples and rubbed. Suddenly, she looked up as if she had just thought of something.

"Fisherman a knot is he," she said.

She looked in her money belt to see if she had a pen or a pencil. She found a black marker.

On her hand she wrote the words: "Fisherman a knot is he."

Then it hit her!

"Oh my gosh!" she said. "No wonder. I know why we haven't been able to figure this out."

"Why?" Brooksie asked excitedly.

"The machine talks backwards."

"Huh?" Becky asked.

"It's backwards," Stephanie said. "It's saying, 'He is not a fisherman.' It wasn't 'knot,' like a knot in a rope, but 'not,' like he 'ain't' a fisherman."

Brooksie covered her mouth.

"Ooooh, you shouldn't say ain't," she said.

"He is not a fisherman," Kenny said out loud. He looked at Stephanie and added, "But what does that mean? You don't suppose it's about the little boy, do you?"

"I don't know what it means," Stephanie said.

She looked out the window. The idea seemed preposterous — that an ancient record player, perhaps fifty years old, would talk about a young boy.

But after her encounter with the little boy, Stephanie was not sure what to believe. Lots of impossible things had happened. The boy had appeared in the window, then vanished. Her hand had gone through him as if he were made of air.

Who was to say what was possible any more?

She desperately wanted things to return to

normal. She did not want to believe that this ancient machine was actually talking about something that was going on right now.

"I don't know," she said. "Maybe it's just part of a song or something."

"A song?" Brooksie asked, incredulously. "What kind of a song is that? I'm telling you, that thing is talking to us."

"You could be right," Stephanie said. "What spooks me is that it plays without the needle working. I think we should just go."

"FISHERMAN . . . A . . . NOT . . . IS . . . HE!" the record player said again.

"All right, we got it," Stephanie said. She tried to stop the record from spinning with her hand, but it kept moving.

"Let's just go," Kenny agreed.

But when Becky opened the door, something downstairs rattled. All of them heard it.

"It's probably the bats," Kenny said. "Don't worry about it. They're in the little room and the door is closed."

"You go first," Becky told him.

Kenny started towards the stairs. Something rattled again. He looked over the railing but could not see anything.

BANG! BANG! BANG!

Kenny ran back up the stairs and pushed the girls back inside the room.

"What was that?" Stephanie said. She trembled a little, but she told herself she was not going to cry again.

Then they heard it again: BANG! BANG BANG!

"I have no idea what that is," Kenny whispered. " Let's stay up here for a little while."

"I want to go," Stephanie said. "I want to get out of here. I don't want to be here anymore."

"Neither do I, Steph," Kenny admitted. "But we have to stay until we're sure it's safe to go downstairs."

"What if it's never safe?" Stephanie asked. Kenny had no answer.

The three girls huddled in a corner on the floor.

Kenny sat by the door trying to listen for any movement downstairs.

The only sound in the room was the crackling of the lantern.

## Chapter Fourteen

"Kenny, do you hear anything?" Stephanie asked.

Kenny pressed his ear to the door, then turned around and shook his head.

Suddenly it seemed very quiet in the lighthouse. The silence seemed to echo and bounce and grow even more quiet. The girls held their breath. Even the bats seemed to be taking a break.

"You think the coast is clear?" Stephanie asked.

"I don't know," Kenny said. "You think I should go check?"

Stephanie hesitated before answering. She did not want Kenny to run into trouble, but there was no other way of knowing if it was safe to leave. And she had to protect the younger girls.

"Yes," she said. "But be careful."

Kenny opened the door slowly and peeked out. He opened the door a little wider, and slipped out. He walked down the steps gingerly so the soles of his sneakers would not squeak.

Still, his footsteps rang through the silence. The girls heard them grow more and more faint as Kenny descended the stairs.

Soon they heard his footsteps running back up the stairs.

"Looks like the coast is clear," he said as he entered the room.

The girls were standing by the phonograph. Kenny waited for one of them to say something.

Instead, the record player spoke again:

"SWIM . . . YOU . . . CAN?" it said, in the oily male voice. "SWIM . . . YOU . . . CAN? . . . SWIM . . . YOU . . . CAN?"

"It's been saying that for a while now," Stephanie said. "I think it wants to know if we can swim."

"If we can swim?" Kenny asked.

"I think that's what it's asking," Stephanie

71

said. "It's just backwards."

"But that doesn't make any sense," Becky said. "Why would it want to know if we can swim? Why?"

"And it said he's not a fisherman," added Brooksie.

"None of that makes any sense to me," Becky said.

Stephanie said nothing. First, the boy had vanished into thin air when he was outside of the window. Then, when she tried to touch him, it seemed like he was *made* of thin air. And now the record player wanted to know if they could swim.

What was going on inside this lighthouse?

Whatever it was, she was not sure she even wanted to understand it.

"Is it all right to go now?" Stephanie asked.

"I think so," Kenny said. "I didn't see anything out of the ordinary downstairs."

"Nothing out of the ordinary!" Stephanie exclaimed. "Everything in this place is out of the ordinary."

"DOWN FALLING IS BRIDGE ISLAND

FERN!" the phonograph yelled. The record had picked up speed. "DOWN FALLING IS BRIDGE ISLAND FERN! DOWN FALLING IS BRIDGE IS-LAND FERN!"

"Look at it!" Brooksie said. "It's going crazy!" She tried to stop the record with her hand, but it continued to spin furiously.

"What's it saying now?" she asked. "Did you guys catch that?"

"DOWN FALLING IS BRIDGE ISLAND FERN!" it said, over and over and over. "DOWN FALLING IS BRIDGE ISLAND FERN! DOWN FALLING IS BRIDGE ISLAND FERN!"

"The bridge! It's talking about the bridge!" Brooksie said.

Stephanie, who had already reached the door in her eagerness to leave, walked back to the record player. The needle was still in its place and the turntable was spinning.

She stared at it in horror.

"DOWN FALLING IS BRIDGE ISLAND FERN!" the machine yelled.

"Did it say Fern Island Bridge is falling down?"

Stephanie asked. "This is really scaring me."

Stephanie walked over to the table and sank into a chair, facing the lantern. She put her head down and tried to concentrate.

The bridge had not fallen down, she told herself. So what did this mean?

Becky and Brooksie started to argue, interrupting her thoughts. Maybe the tension was getting to them.

"What difference does it make what this funky old thing is saying?" Becky asked, in a snobby-sounding voice.

"It makes a big difference," Brooksie said. "If it's talking, there has to be a reason. Have you ever seen a record player talk before?"

"Whatever you say," Becky sneered.

Just then, they heard a loud thud downstairs.

With that, the phonograph abruptly stopped spinning.

# **Chapter Fifteen**

"Oh no!" Stephanie yelled. "What was that? Come on you guys, let's go! Now!"

She opened the door. They heard a crash.

"AHHHH!" Brooksie yelled. She looked as if she was beginning to panic.

"Be quiet," said Stephanie. "Take a deep breath and calm down. We'll be OK in a minute. Let's just leave."

Suddenly, they heard another crash — this one in the room where they stood. Shards of glass tinkled to the floor around them.

They whirled around. A hole gaped in a shattered window.

Then they all screamed.

Bats streamed in through the broken window and darkened the air of the room. Swarms of them darted and screeched and flapped their hideous black wings.

The children covered their heads with their arms and ducked onto the floor, trying not to cut themselves on the daggers of broken glass.

Then the bats swarmed out the window and flew off into the sky in a terrible dark cloud.

The girls huddled together on the floor with their arms around each other's shoulders.

"We're never going to get out of here," Stephanie said. She was near tears, and she shivered like a leaf in the wind. Her lip quivered, but she kept her promise to herself not to cry again.

Brooksie started to sob. Becky was biting her lip, trying not to cry. She looked at her big sister for help.

"Kenny, how are we going to get out of here?" Stephanie asked.

Kenny looked badly shaken. He had lost his confident look, and seemed to have long ago lost his taste for adventure.

He was silent for a moment, and when he spoke, his voice shook.

"I think we just have to make a run for it," he said. "But I have to tell you something. I think there's someone — or some*thing* — in that little room below."

"Some*thing*?" Stephanie asked. "Like what?"

"I have no idea. When I looked in there before and found the bats — which I did *not* let out, by the way, I couldn't see anything in there. But I heard footsteps. And the door opened by itself."

"We have to get out of here," Stephanie said. "Whatever it takes. I do not want to be here another second."

"I agree," Kenny said. "But I don't want us to all get hauled into that secret room by something weird, either."

Stephanie started hiccupping.

"Steph, why don't you sit down for a few minutes?" Kenny said. "Let's all calm down a minute, if that's possible, and figure out what's our best chance of getting out of here."

Stephanie sat down on the floor. She held her breath and counted to ten. She took another deep breath and counted to ten again. When the hiccups were gone, she closed her eyes and tried to imagine all the things she liked the most in the world — eating ice cream and flying kites and hugging her teddy bear at night when she was alone in her room, and no one could see.

What she wouldn't do for a banana split right now, she thought. Alone in her room with her teddy, and maybe a kite flying on a string through the open window.

She opened her eyes and noticed the newspapers on the floor next to her. Kenny was deep in thought, plotting their escape. Stephanie tried reading some of the newspaper stories to distract herself.

Becky noticed and came over and sat next to Stephanie.

"That's the other weird thing about this place," Becky said. "The articles in those newspapers are in another language or something."

"That's not that strange," Kenny said. "They have papers in other countries, you know."

"I know that," Becky answered. "But these seem to be papers from around here, but the words are not English."

BANG! BANG! BANG! They were suddenly startled by more noises from down the stairs.

"Kenny, what are we going to do?" Stephanie asked.

Kenny ignored the question. He looked as if he had no answer, and he was running out of comforting things to say. He also looked as if he might be running out of courage.

The record player gurgled. The turntable started spinning again. Each spin was faster than the last. But it said nothing.

Stephanie picked up the newspaper that had the picture of the woman holding the child and the fishing pole. It looked like a regular newspaper, except that it was yellow and brittle with age.

Other than that, it reminded her of her hometown paper — headlines and articles and photographs, all laid out so they fit exactly together.

Stephanie studied the articles, trying to make sense of them. But Becky was right. They were incomprehensible — just random words, pure gibberish.

The phonograph spun and spun without uttering a word. Kenny sat by the door, trying to pick a good time to make a break for it. Becky and Brooksie sat on the floor, not saying a word.

Stephanie looked up at the record player, wondering why it was so silent all of a sudden. Why wasn't it talking backwards anymore?

Then it hit her!

She picked up an article and scanned down to the bottom of the page, where it ended. She read the last word first, then the next-to-last word, and then the third word from the end.

The articles were like the messages from the phonograph. They were backwards!

"You guys," she shouted. "This is English! But the sentences are backwards!"

"They're backwards, too?" Kenny asked.

"Yeah," Stephanie replied.

"What does it say?"

"Kenny, there's a zillion stories here," she said.

"Well, pick one," he said.

Stephanie took the page she had scanned and put it on her lap. Her eyes focused on the front page story next to the photograph of the mother and her child.

She read a few sentences to herself, her eyes narrowing as she concentrated on reading backwards.

Then her mouth fell open.

"It's about a little boy," she said, "who died while he was fishing."

# Chapter Sixteen

"And?" Becky asked impatiently. "What else does the story say?"

Stephanie took a deep breath and started reading, beginning with the end of the article and working her way to the top:

*"A 7-year-old boy apparently died Sunday when the bridge he was sitting on collapsed and he fell into the sea, Fern Island police said.*

*"The boy, Mike Taylor, was sitting on the bridge fishing when it mysteriously split in two, dumping the boy backwards into the water, police said.*

*"Although police divers have not been able to locate the body, a police spokesman said officers assume the boy drowned.*

*"The boy's parents, Evelyn and James Taylor,*

told police that he did not know how to swim and was rarely allowed to go to Fern Island by himself. Because he had recently gotten good grades at school, his father had allowed him to go fishing by himself on Sunday.

"Police said they will continue to search for the boy's body, but they are not optimistic they will find it. Police divers reported that the ocean currents were particularly strong on Sunday, and police said that chances of finding the body grow more remote with each passing hour.

"Evelyn Taylor said that her son fell in love with fishing when he was five years old and accompanied his father on a fishing trip. He was a skilled angler, she said, often bringing home delicious catches for her to cook.

"She decribed her son as a shy boy, somewhat of a loner, who seemed happiest when fishing the sea by himself.

"Fern Island Police Chief John White said his department was saddened by the boy's 'tragic death' and 'will help the family anyway we can.'

" 'It's ironic that what he loved the most in

the world ended up causing his death,' White said. 'I guess you can say that he died doing what he loved. But, still, it's very difficult to think about a 7-year-old in those terms.'

"The investigation into the cause of the bridge's collapse will continue, police said. The 12-year-old bridge connecting Fern Island to the mainland has never had any previous structural problems, officials said.

" 'It's as if the bridge had a mind of its own,' one official said. 'There is no apparent cause for the collapse yet. But we won't rest until we figure this out.'

"Officials said that, without knowing what caused the collapse, it is impossible to say whether the Fern Island Bridge will ever open again."

Stephanie lifted the page and pointed to the picture.

"The picture next to it is of the mother and the boy," she said.

Kenny reached over, and Stephanie handed the paper to him.

"I don't want to cross that bridge ever again,"

Brooksie said.

"Does it say when that happened?" Becky asked.

Kenny searched the newspaper.

"I can't find a date," he said. "The top of this page is really smudged."

He handed the paper back to Stephanie. She took it, and began studying the picture more carefully. The boy in the picture, Mike Taylor, looked a lot like the little boy in the lighthouse — the one that had vanished into thin air. The one whose arms aren't real.

But she didn't mention it to Kenny. He had never seen the boy face-to-face like she had. And she had promised herself she was not going to tell him about her encounter with the boy until he had kept his agreement to leave the island.

You never knew when Kenny might get brave again, and decide he really wanted to stay in this eerie place another hour so *he* could see the boy, too.

"I wonder if they ever found the boy's body," Brooksie said.

"It doesn't sound like there was much hope for that," Becky said.

"There's something really odd about this story," Stephanie said. "But I can't put my finger on it. Maybe it's just freaking me out because we're here."

"It's sad," Becky said. "Poor kid. Can you imagine if that bridge would have split open when we were crossing it?"

"No, I can't imagine that," Brooksie said. "And I don't want to. Do you mind?"

"At least, we know how to swim," Becky continued.

"Don't you guys think it's very weird that a bridge would just split open like that?" Stephanie asked.

"Maybe there was more to it," Becky said. "Maybe they figured out why it collapsed later on."

"But there's something really, really weird about this," she said.

Stephanie paused, not wanting to scare the younger ones, then plunged ahead. She still wouldn't tell Kenny what had actually happened when she met the boy. But they were all in this together. They all deserved to know what she was thinking.

"The boy in this picture," she said, "looks a lot like the boy in this lighthouse. A *lot* like him."

"But this story is so old," Kenny said. "It can't be him."

Suddenly, they heard a crashing noise downstairs, followed by a loud, shrill sound.

"That," Stephanie said solemnly, "does not sound like bats to me."

# **Chapter Seventeen**

Kenny reached for Stephanie's hand and held it.

Her palms were sweaty, and so were his. She kept biting her bottom lip. So did he. Each sensed that the other was scared and needed help.

He let go of Stephanie and walked over to the door and opened it. He looked down the staircase, and reported that he could see nothing — no bats, no strange little boys, nothing.

The secret door was still open, he said, but from the top of the staircase, he could not tell for certain whether anyone was down there in the shadows or not.

The booming had stopped. So had the loud, shrill sound.

And the silence was almost scarier than the

noise.

Kenny walked back into the room. Becky and Brooksie were still discussing the newspaper article. Maybe they were too young to realize just how scary this situation really was. They were trapped by forces they could not identify — held hostage by the unknown.

Stephanie had sat back down on the floor. She sat with her legs crossed, and she waggled one foot nervously.

"I think there is a connection," Brooksie said, working this new puzzle over in her mind. "I just don't know what it is."

"A connection to what?" Becky said. "I don't see any evidence of how any of this could make sense or be related."

Evidence, Stephanie thought to herself. Her kid sister, the detective, needed some evidence.

"Don't you think it's, like, way too strange that the record player is trying to tell us things about the bridge — and then we find out that a long time ago the bridge collapsed?" Brooksie asked.

"And a boy drowned," Stephanie added.

"Don't forget that."

"But how do you connect those things?" Becky asked.

Kenny interrupted.

"You guys, I don't see anything down there," he said. "I think we should make a run for it."

"BURN . . . MUST . . . LANTERN . . . THE!" the record player said. "BURN . . . MUST . . . LANTERN . . . THE! . . . BURN . . . MUST . . . LANTERN . . . THE!"

"What does that *mean*?" Becky asked.

"BURN . . . MUST . . . LANTERN . . . THE!" the machine repeated, even louder.

"The lantern must burn!" Brooksie exclaimed. "That's what it said. The lantern must burn!"

They all turned to look at the lantern. It was burning on top of the table, the flame flickering brightly.

"This gives me the creeps!" Stephanie said. "Kenny's right. Let's make a run for it."

"This is really freaky," Brooksie added. "I knew this thing was trying to tell us something. Why does the lantern have to burn? What does that have to do with anything?"

"Look, let's just go," Stephanie said. "We may not get another chance."

"BURN MUST LANTERN THE!" the machine said, faster this time. "BURN MUST LANTERN THE! BURN MUST LANTERN THE! BURN MUST LANTERN THE! BURN MUST LANTERN THE!"

The record player was spinning out of control. It's voice sounded more and more frantic.

Stephanie walked to the closet and slammed the door. The phonograph was still buzzing, but the words were muffled.

She walked to the table and stood next to the lantern. She thought of the little boy fishing by the bridge with the lantern next to him. Then she thought of the picture in the newspaper.

Kenny looked at her oddly, and she knew a strange look must have come over her face.

"Steph," he asked. "Do you really think that the little boy who drowned could be the little boy we followed here?"

Stephanie scratched her head.

"I don't know," she said. "If he died, how could it be him? But then, how did he disappear on us like that? Does he have magical powers or something?"

"What if he didn't really die?" Kenny asked. "What if they just never found him?"

A shiver ran through Stephanie's body. She remembered how she had touched the boy's shoulder and felt nothing but air.

"And the messages," Brooksie said. "The first one asked us if we could swim. Then it said that he is not a fisherman. Then it said the bridge was falling down. And now it's telling us that the lantern must burn. I think the messages are about the boy. The boy couldn't swim and the bridge collapsed."

"Yeah, but the boy *was* fishing when he died," Becky said. "Why would it say he's not a fisherman? And the lantern part just doesn't make any sense."

"If he's not a fisherman . . ." Stephanie said slowly, and another shiver ran down her spine, " . . . then he must be something else. And I don't really want to know what that is."

Becky's eyes opened wide, and she gazed at

her big sister in astonishment.

"Steph," she said. "I thought you told me you don't believe in ghosts. I believed you when you told me there weren't any such things."

She looked accusingly at Stephanie, as if she were a liar.

"Well?" she demanded. "Do you believe there's a ghost in this very room? Watching our every move? Listening to what we're saying?"

"That's it!" Stephanie yelled. "Let's go! Now!"

She ran to the door and held it open. Kenny left first. Brooksie scooted out after him.

"Come *on*, Becky!" Stephanie yelled, standing at the door.

Becky looked like she was in a trance. She walked slowly to the table, picked up the lantern, and inspected it.

She had tried before to blow out the flame and failed. Slowly, she set the lantern down and started to walk away.

Then she stopped.

She moved back to the table, bent over, closed

her eyes, and took a deep breath.

Stephanie watched from the doorway, spell-bound. If this was a magic lantern, she wanted to know.

Becky blew with all her might. The flame went out.

Quickly, she strode over to the door and started down the stairs. Stephanie closed the door behind them.

# Chapter Eighteen

The four of them piled down the stairs, hoping to escape the lighthouse before anything else happened.

Kenny had nearly reached the front door when a terrible, blood-curdling shriek stopped them all in their tracks. It was coming from upstairs!

The wailing grew louder and louder. Stephanie's blood ran cold. All of them stood motionless, frozen with fear.

The wail sounded so awful — filled with pain and dispair.

Kenny pulled himself together and opened the front door.

They heard a roar and a huge whirring of wings coming from the room under the stairs.

The bats! Hundreds of them flew out of the

secret room in an awful black cloud, screeching and darting and beating their wings. They surrounded the girls, swarming around them so thickly they could not even see each other.

"AGGGHHHHHHH!" the girls yelled. They threw their arms over their heads to keep the wings from slapping them in the face.

Kenny's mouth hung open. He looked for something to swing at the bats, to beat them back, but he couldn't even see six inches in front of him.

Stephanie, Brooksie and Becky huddled together. Becky cried loudly, but her sobs were nearly drowned out by the whirring of wings. Brooksie closed her eyes and prayed.

Stephanie ground her teeth.

"Kenny, where are you?" she yelled. She was not sure he could hear her voice over the thrashing of the wings.

"Over here!" he yelled. "Don't move! And stick together!"

Lightning flashed, turning the inside of the lighthouse as bright as day for a second, and casting shadows of hundreds of bats on the walls. Thunder crashed.

Suddenly, the cloud of bats started flying toward the room behind the staircase. Like a great black plume of smoke, they disappeared through the door and into the room.

Kenny ran to the front door and pushed on it.

It was stuck fast.

"What's wrong?" Stephanie asked. "Won't it open?"

Kenny shook his head. He turned the knob and pushed harder, shoving his shoulder against the door for leverage.

Still, it would not open.

"We're trapped," Stephanie wailed. "I told you we should never have come here!"

"Shut the door to the little room!" Kenny shouted. "At least let's keep the bats away from us!"

Stephanie ran behind the staircase and slammed the door. Then she ran to the front door to help Kenny push.

Together, they put their shoulders against the door and shoved.

The door inched open a crack.

"Becky, Brooksie, come help us!" Stephanie yelled.

The four of them pressed their shoulders to the door.

"On the count of three," Kenny said. "One, two, three!"

They pushed with all their might, yelling and grunting with the effort. Stephanie pushed so hard her feet slid on the floor, and she had to scramble for traction.

"Keep pushing!" she shouted. "We have to get out of here!"

They yelled again with effort and leaned against the door as hard as they could.

It flew open, sending them sprawling outside the lighthouse.

Quickly, they picked themselves up and sprinted to the fence where they had left their bicycles.

They were gone!

"Oh, no!" Kenny cried.

"We've got to find them!" Stephanie shouted.

Lightning flashed, throwing the lighthouse into sharp relief. Thunder crashed.

Stephanie began to run around to the other side of the lighthouse. The others followed.

Lightning flashed again — and in the sudden light, she saw the bikes. They lay in a heap on the ground, full of sand and dirt.

"Over here!" she yelled.

They picked up the bikes, jumped aboard, and pedaled away as fast as they could, leaving the lighthouse behind.

The wind blew. Black clouds billowed in, but it had not yet started to rain.

Kenny led the way. The trail led into the woods, but they were not sure it was the same trail they had followed on the way to the lighthouse.

That calm ride — when the sun had been out, the winds had been calm, and they had chased the little boy on purpose — seemed so long ago it was almost like something from another lifetime.

Kenny stopped uncertainly. Stephanie pulled up next to him.

"Does this look familiar?" she asked.

"Not really," Kenny said. "But I really wasn't paying attention. I was just following that boy."

"It doesn't seem like we came this way," Stephanie said.

"There can't be too many different ways to get to the bridge," Kenny said. "This island isn't that big. We'll find it."

They continued to ride deeper into the woods. Becky and Brooksie did not talk.

"I don't like it in here," Stephanie said. "Why don't we backtrack a bit and figure out how we got here?"

"You want to backtrack toward the light-house?" Kenny asked.

"Uh, no, not really," Stephanie said. "I just thought we could find some other route."

Kenny was right, Stephanie thought. Anything was better than the lighthouse.

They rode on, as fast as they could pedal on the trail. The woods were dark. The wind blew fiercely, bending the trees and blowing their hair.

All at once, crawling down the trunk of a tree, Stephanie saw a snake.

She gasped, and almost swerved off the trail.

Then she saw another snake slithering along

the ground. In a panic, she looked ahead — and saw more snakes squirming along the trail.

"KENNY!" she yelled. "Don't you see them?"

"I see them!" he yelled. "What should we do?"

"We have to turn around!" Brooksie cried, almost hysterically.

"Turn around?" Becky said. "Back to the lighthouse? Are you crazy?"

"We can't go back," Stephanie said. "Just ride as fast as you can. We can get by the snakes. It's our only chance."

They pedaled furiously. Kenny was in front, riding for his life. The girls worked hard to keep up.

Stephanie let Becky and Brooksie ride ahead of her. Kenny was so scared that he was riding ahead with no concern for the others. But she had to take care of the younger girls. She did not want them to get lost.

Suddenly, she thought she heard someone behind her.

She turned around, but saw nothing. It must have been a tree branch rustling in the wind, she thought.

Then someone tapped her on the shoulder.

She turned around wildly, almost falling off her bike.

She saw no one. She was starting to hate the woods as much as she had hated the lighthouse.

The deeper into the woods they rode, the more snakes they saw. They dangled from tree branches and slithered across the trail. But at least they seemed to be keeping to themselves.

Stephanie felt someone pull her hair. Again she turned around. She saw no one. She gripped her handlebars tightly, gritted her teeth, and rode on.

Then she heard someone running behind her. She could make out distinctly the sound of the footsteps, the snapping of twigs, the panting of someone running hard and out of breath.

When she looked, she saw no one — just the forest trail and the dangling snakes and the tree branches waving and bowing in the wind.

"Kenny, do you see anything ahead of us?" she yelled.

"The bridge!" he hollered back. "I can see the
bridge!"

# Chapter Nineteen

The Fern Island Bridge appeared tiny in the distance. Black clouds scudded across the sky. Fat raindrops spat in their faces.

"Thank God!" Stephanie said. "I thought we'd never make it back."

Kenny and Stephanie stopped to allow the younger girls to catch their breath. But they did not want to wait long. It looked as if the clouds might burst at any moment, drenching them with rain.

"Come on, let's go," Stephanie said. "We don't want to have to work our way across that bridge in the rain.

Kenny hopped on his bike and pedaled off toward the bridge. Stephanie allowed herself a little smile. Kenny had been the most eager of any of them to come — and now he seemed to be the most eager to leave.

She motioned to Becky and Brooksie to come along, then mounted her bike and rode off after Kenny.

The weather was dark, but her mood light. The troubles of the lighthouse were behind her. Up ahead, beyond the bridge, she could see the mainland. She would soon be on familiar ground.

As she rode, she noticed a shadow to her right. But when she looked, there was nobody there. Nor was there any sunshine to cast a shadow.

Then she saw a shadow on her left. She looked again. Again, she saw nothing.

She gripped the handlebars more tightly. Her light and airy mood vanished.

"Let's ride a little faster," she called to the younger girls, and they pedaled on with new determination.

Then she felt someone touch her on the shoulder. She ignored it, thinking she had been brushed by a windblown branch or, perhaps, a pine cone.

Then something tapped her on the head. Wildly, she brushed whatever it was away with her hand.

Kenny sped along, standing on the pedals, far ahead of the rest of them. He turned and looked back over his shoulder at them.

"WHAT?" he yelled.

"What what?" Stephanie shouted.

"What do you want?" Kenny said.

"I don't want anything," Stephanie said.

"Who called me?"

"You're hearing things," Stephanie said.

Kenny bent low over the handlebars and pedaled like a madman. Then he twisted back to face them again, riding forwards but looking backwards.

"Did you guys hear that?" Kenny asked.

"Did we hear what?" Stephanie asked.

"Never mind," Kenny said. He turned back around and rode as if he were being chased by demons.

He stopped, however, and waited for them at the bridge. Stephanie caught up, panting, and stopped to wait for Becky and Brooksie.

Stephanie looked at the bridge with mixed emotions. Crossing that bridge had led to the most bizarre and terrifying day of their lives.

But it was also the way home, the route back to safety.

"I am so glad," Stephanie whispered, half to herself.

"Me too," Kenny admitted. "Me, too."

He stood and stared at the bridge, which swayed slightly in the wind of the approaching storm.

"You think the boy in that story is really the same boy we saw?" he asked.

Stephanie wasn't sure whether she should answer. She had promised herself she would not tell Kenny about her encounter with the boy until they were off the island.

She took a look at his face. One glance told her he wouldn't go back to look for the boy no matter what she said.

Becky and Brooksie rode up as she responded.

"I do," she said. "I think he *lives* in the lighthouse — and I think he may be a ghost. Or maybe he has some kind of strange powers or something. When I met him — remember I wouldn't tell you? I tried to touch him and I couldn't feel a thing. My hand went right through him, like air. And remember when he vanished in the window? And think about all that weird stuff with the record player and the article and the lantern."

"Don't be ridiculous," Becky said. "I blew the lantern out before we left. And nothing happened. See? We're all still here and we're fine."

"You *what*?" Kenny asked. "Are you crazy or something?"

"What's the big deal?" Becky continued. "Nothing happened."

Now that they were at the bridge, her courage and bluster seemed to have returned.

"Nothing happened?" Kenny exlaimed. "What about the yelling and the bats and the lights?"

"And the door wouldn't open!" Brooksie added.

"Oh come on," Becky said. "We were hearing things all afternoon in the lighthouse, when the lantern was on. What makes you think that all of that happened because the lantern was off?"

"The record player asked us not to blow it out," Kenny said. His face was dead serious — and,

Stephanie thought, very pale.

"It also told us that he is not a fisherman whoever he is," Becky continued. "And it also asked us if we could swim and it told us that the bridge is falling down. Does it look like that bridge is falling down?"

All four of them turned to looked at the bridge and paused. A wave of relief swept over them. They all started laughing at the same time.

"Actually, it does," Brooksie said. "Hey, let's stop gabbing and cross it already. I can't wait to get home."

"We have to be careful," Kenny said.

"Yeah, especially now that we know that it collapsed and a little boy drowned," Brooksie said.

"That was *ages* ago," Becky said.

"We really don't know how long ago it was," Stephanie said. "Just be careful. I know you think you're Wonder Woman, but just be careful."

"Should I go first?" Kenny asked, a little bit too eagerly.

"No," Stephanie said. "I'd feel better if you were last. Let's let Brooksie and Becky go first."

Suddenly, Kenny spun around.

"Who said that?" he cried out.

The others looked at him strangely.

"Are you OK?" Stephanie asked. "Did you hear what I just said?"

"Uh, yeah, sure," Kenny said, shakily. "I'll do whatever you want."

"Becky, you go first," Stephanie said. It was clear that she was now in charge of this expedition.

"You want *me* to go first?" Becky asked. "You remember what happened to me the last time?"

"Take it slow," Stephanie said. "If you hadn't been such a show-off, you would have made it fine, like the rest of us."

Becky made a face, but she pushed her bike onto the bridge and walked slowly over the planks. The bridge creaked under her and swayed slightly.

"You're doing fine," Stephanie yelled. "Keep it up, you're almost there."

"I can't believe this thing once split open in half," Brooksie whispered to Stephanie.

"Stop thinking about that," Stephanie said. "We're going to be fine."

Stephanie stayed calm. She knew it was important. But, inside, she was in turmoil. Images of the lighthouse, the strange little boy, the phonograph, and the lantern flashed through her mind.

And she wondered whether it would matter that they had disobeyed the record player, and had blown out the lantern.

Becky crossed safely to the mainland. Stephanie signaled for Brooksie start crossing.

"I'm really nervous," Brooksie said. Stephanie patted her on the back.

"Just go slowly and don't think about anything else," she said.

"And remember you have to stay over to this side. You don't want to get caught between the planks."

Reluctantly, Brooksie started walking her bike across the bridge. Kenny stood next to Stephanie, who had her eyes fixed on Brooksie.

Suddenly, Kenny whirled around again. Then he looked at Stephanie with pleading eyes.

"Steph," he said, "Please tell me you heard that!"

"Heard what?" she responded without looking

at him.

"You didn't hear that voice calling my name?"

"Kenny, don't tell me you're hallucinating — now that it's all over."

"Steph, I swear," Kenny said. "I heard it when we were riding and I'm hearing it now. I'm not crazy."

"That lighthouse has made us all crazy," Stephanie said. "Let's just concentrate on getting home."

Brooksie made it safely to the other side.

Stephanie went next. She pushed her bike onto the bridge and tried to force any thoughts of the lighthouse out of her mind. It was not easy. She kept picturing the bridge opening up and letting her slide into the ocean.

Kenny didn't wait for Stephanie to make it to the other side before he began to cross the bridge. Just as she was half-way across, Stephanie felt the bridge jog and waver, and she looked back to see that Kenny was already pushing his bike across.

Fear shone wildly in his eyes.

"WHAT?" he shouted turning around. "WHAT?"

"Kenny," Stephanie said softly. "Kenny, it's all right. We're almost safe."

"WHAT?" Kenny yelled again. *"Please stop calling my name!"*

He whirled again, looking around crazily, forgetting to watch where he was going.

He wobbled and veered and turned his wheel by mistake. His front tire got stuck between two planks. He was on the wrong side of the bridge!

"Darn!" Kenny yelled.

He yanked ferociously on his bike. It would not budge.

"Aaaaggghhh!"  Kenny yelled. He yanked again, with all his might. The bridge bounced from his efforts. Stephanie looked back at him. He looked as if he was losing his mind.

"Kenny," she called. "Kenny, you have to move to the other side of the bridge. You're right where Becky got stuck on the way over."

"I know!" Kenny yelled. He heaved and pushed and finally jerked the bike loose.

He started forward, looking up at the girls. Then he spun around again.

"WHAT? WHAT? WHAT?" he called. He was close to tears.

His lurching and turning made the bridge sway from side to side. He gripped his bike tightly and waited for it to stop.

But the bridge continued to move from side to side, like a swing.

And the planks of the bridge started to spread apart.

Stephanie scrambled off the bridge and looked back.

"Kenny, hold on!" she cried. Becky and Brooksie stood next to her holding hands.

Was this, after all, what the record player had really meant? Was the Fern Island Bridge going to fall down once again?

## Chapter Twenty

"What a nightmare," Stephanie whispered to herself. "Why did we ever do this?"

Three of them were safe. Kenny was so close.

But the planks of the Fern Island Bridge were starting to splay apart. And Kenny was beginning to panic. Stephanie knew she had to stay calm.

"Kenny, hold on tight," she called. She felt like screaming it, but she said it the way a mother might talk to a child about to get on a carousel.

Kenny looked at her with frightened eyes, but he seemed to hear what she was saying. He tightened his grip on his bicycle and tried to center himself on the bridge, hoping to balance the weight.

The bridge swayed from left to right over and over again. Kenny clung to his bike, standing right at the center of the bridge.

The bridge rocked and bucked and swayed. Then the motions subsided and became more and more gentle until at last the bridge was completely still.

Kenny looked relieved. He wiped his forehead with a sleeve, took a deep breath and pushed his bike forward very slowly.

Suddenly, without turning around, he shouted.

"I'M NOT TURNING AROUND," he yelled. "NO MATTER WHO YOU ARE!"

He walked with deliberate steps, trying to keep the bridge from rocking. He seemed to be gaining confidence.

"I'M NOT ANSWERING!" he shouted. He kept his eyes riveted on the land at the edge of the bridge.

"I DON'T HEAR YOU!" he yelled. "SO STOP YELLING MY NAME."

He looked at the girls.

"I suppose you didn't hear that, either," he said grimly. "Well, neither did I. I'm just losing my mind, that's all. No problem."

Stephanie smiled in spite of herself. She was

proud of him, and the way he had pulled himself together. He could be a fool sometimes, but he was her best friend.

And he was going to make it!

She felt as if all the tears she had held inside for so long were going to well up in her eyes now and stream down her cheeks.

Kenny stepped off the bridge and breathed deeply several times. Stephanie ran up and hugged him, crying onto his shoulder. He was shaking, but he had made it.

"Finally, we can go home!" Stephanie said. She wiped the tears from her face.

"Yes, finally," Kenny whispered. "I can't wait to go home and lie down."

Suddenly, his body stiffened.

"Steph, did you hear that?" he asked her in a low tone so that the others could not hear.

"Kenny, stop that," Stephanie said. "You're safe. It's going to rain, and my mom is going to kill me if she finds out I let Becky and Brooksie ride their bikes in the rain."

Kenny got on his bicycle to lead the way home.

He watched the girls mount their bikes before heading out in front of them. The wind gusted cool and wet, signaling the beginning of a rainstorm.

They started riding fast, bent over the handlebars to cut through the wind.

Kenny turned around.

"Did you hear *that*, Steph?" he asked.

She shook her head.

"I was right," Kenny said. "I'm going nuts."

Suddenly an angry male voice boomed across the landscape.

"I SAID WAIT!" it shouted.

All of them jammed on their breaks, nearly toppling into one another. This time, they had all heard it.

Stephanie looked at Kenny and winced. She closed her eyes and said a quick prayer.

"What was that?" Becky whispered to Brooksie. Brooksie bit her lip and shrugged.

Then Stephanie heard someone snicker near her. She looked toward the ocean.

The little boy, wearing his blue jeans and baseball cap, stood under a palmetto tree.

"Oh my gosh, it's him!" Stephanie said. Becky and Brooksie squirmed in their seats. Kenny stood on his pedals and looked at the boy.

"What does he want?" Stephanie asked.

"What is he doing on our side of the bridge?" Brooksie asked.

"What are we going to do, Steph?" Kenny asked. "Should we make a run for it?"

"Yes," Stephanie said. "On the count of three."

"One," she began.

The little boy ran closer to them and stood perfectly straight, his eyes bright and piercing. He held his fishing pole in one hand and his lantern in the other. Stephanie noticed the lantern was lit.

"CAN YOU GUYS SWIM?" he asked.